Grades 1–5 Bassoon

Improve your sight-reading!

Paul Harris

ff MUSIC

Introduction

Being a good sight-reader is so important and it's not difficult at all! If you work through this book carefully – always making sure that you really understand each exercise before you play it – you'll never have problems learning new pieces or doing well at sight-reading in exams!

Using the workbook

1 Rhythmic exercises

Make sure you have grasped these fully before you go on to the melodic exercises: it is vital that you really know how the rhythms work. There are a number of ways to do the exercises, several of which are outlined in Stage 1. Try them all out. Can you think of more ways to do them?

2 Melodic exercises

These exercises use just the notes (and rhythms) for the Stage, and progress gradually. If you want to sight-read fluently and accurately, get into the simple habit of working through each exercise in the following ways before you begin to play it:

- Make sure you understand the rhythm and counting. Clap the exercise through.
- Know what notes you are going to play and the fingering you are going to use.
- Try to hear the piece through in your head. Always play the first note to help.

3 Prepared pieces

Work your way through the questions first, as these will help you to think about, or 'prepare' the piece. Don't begin playing until you are pretty sure you know exactly how the piece goes.

4 Going solo!

It is now up to you to discover the clues in this series of practice pieces. Give yourself about a minute and do your best to understand the piece before you play. Check the rhythms and fingering, and try to hear the piece in your head.

Always remember to feel the pulse and to keep going steadily once you've begun.

Good luck and happy sight-reading!

Terminology:
Bar = measure

Grade 1 Stage 1

Rhythmic exercises

Always practise the rhythmic exercises carefully first. There are different ways
of doing these exercises:
- Your teacher (or a metronome) taps the lower line while you clap or tap
  the upper line.
- You tap the lower line with your foot and clap or tap the upper line.
- You tap one line with one hand and the other line with the other hand on
  a table top or any flat surface.
- You tap the lower line and sing the upper line.

Before you begin each exercise count two bars in – one out loud and one silently.

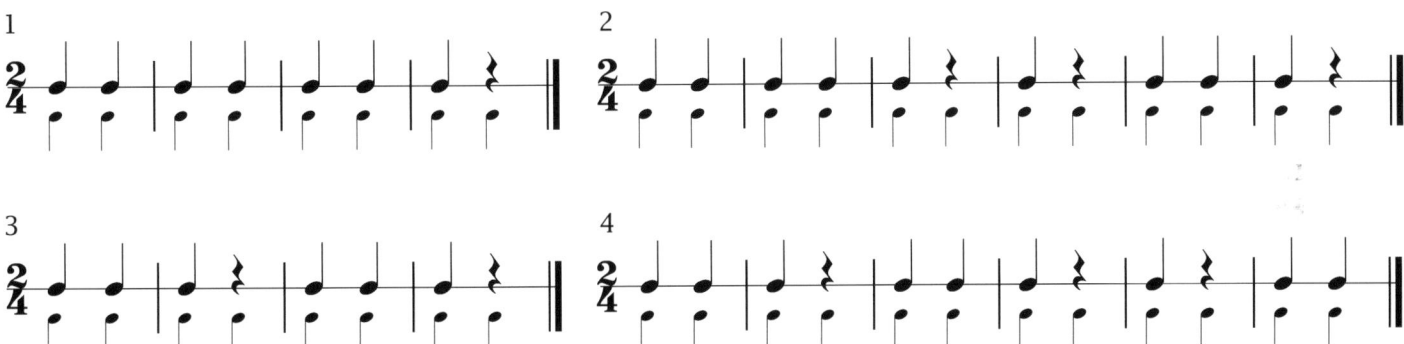

Melodic exercises

Hear each exercise in your head before you play it.

Prepared pieces

1 How many beats are there in each bar? Count six bars aloud, clapping the pulse at the same time.

2 Can you name all the notes in bars 1–3?

3 What do bars 2 and 3 have in common?

4 Play a C (the first note), then hear the piece in your head.

5 How will you put some character into your performance?

1

Lightly

mf

1 What does $\frac{2}{4}$ mean? What is the $\frac{2}{4}$ marking called?

2 Tap the pulse with one hand and the rhythm with the other, on your knees or a flat surface.

3 Are there any repeated melodic patterns?

4 Compare the note in bar 3 with the first note in bar 4.

5 How will you put some character into your performance?

2

Heavily

f

Improvise!

Improvise a 4-bar tune, then a 6-bar tune, beginning with these two bars. Keep it very simple!

Compose!

Compose your own 4-bar tune beginning with these two bars – make the final note an F. Then play your tune.

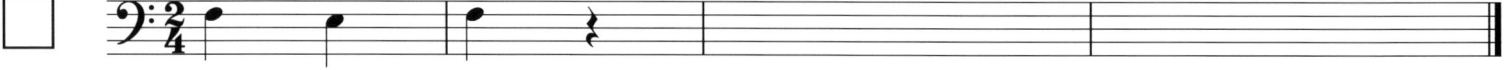

Going solo!

Talk about each piece before you play it. Mention note names, scale
and rhythmic patterns, and the character. After you've played it,
consider how well the music matched your description.

Grade 1   Stage 2

Rhythmic exercises

Always remember to count two bars in.

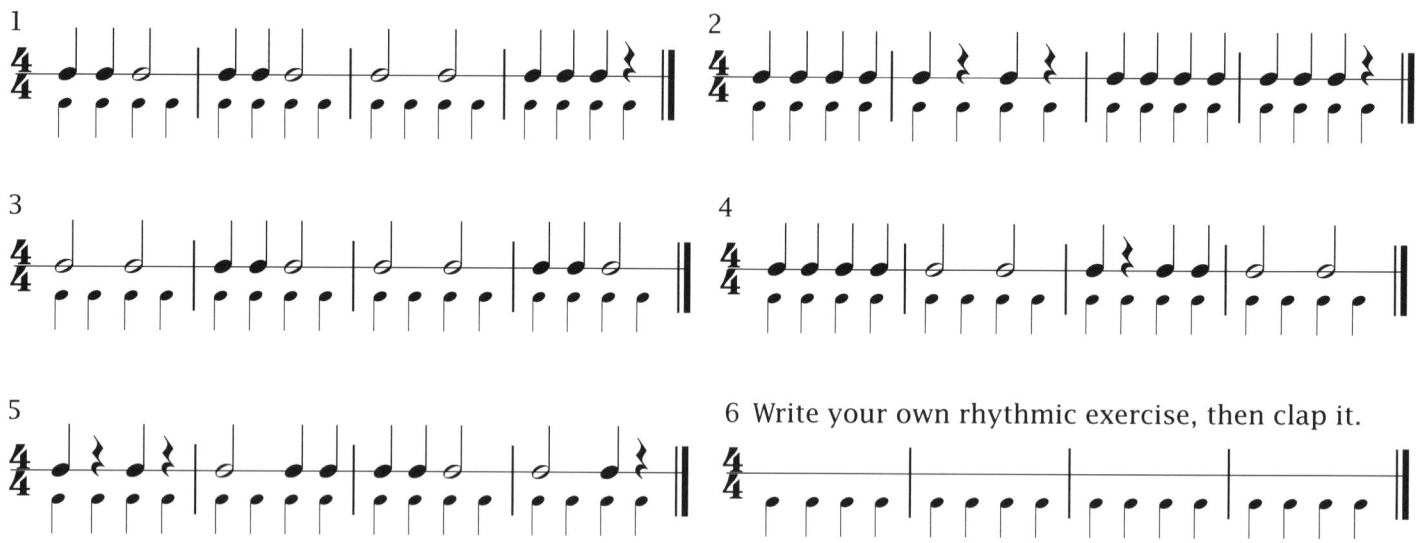

Melodic exercises

Set 1: Exploring F major   First play the scale and arpeggio from notation.

Set 2: Exploring small leaps

Prepared pieces

1 How many beats are there in each bar? Count six bars aloud, clapping the pulse
   at the same time.

2 What is the key? Can you find any scale patterns?

3 Play the highest and lowest notes. What are their names?

4 Play an F (the first note), then hear the piece in your head. Try singing the first two bars.

5 How will you play this piece 'expressively'?

Expressively

1

mf

1 What does $\frac{4}{4}$ mean? Hear a $\frac{4}{4}$ pulse in your head.

2 Tapping the pulse, hear the rhythm in your head. Then clap the rhythm and tap
   the pulse with a foot at the same time.

3 Are there any repeated rhythmic patterns?

4 In which key is this piece? Are any notes affected by the key signature?

5 How will you make the piece sound like a march?

Marching

2

f

Improvise!

Improvise a 4-bar tune, then a 6-bar tune
beginning with these two bars. Remember
to keep it simple.

Compose!

Compose your own 4-bar tune beginning with these two bars. Use some patterns
or ideas from the opening bars and make the final note F. Then play your tune.

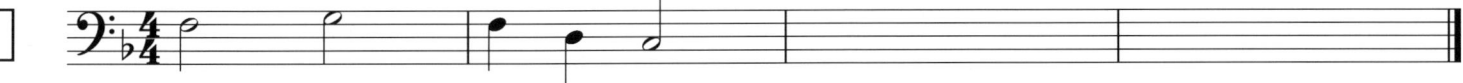

Going solo!

Read through each piece carefully before you play it, hearing it in
your head as best you can. Then count in two bars and think about
how you continue to feel the pulse once you've begun.

Grade 1   Stage 3

G major
Slurs

Rhythmic exercises

Always remember to count two bars in.

Melodic exercises

Set 1: Exploring G major First play the scale and arpeggio from notation.

Set 2: Exploring two-note slurs and quavers

Prepared pieces

> **1** What are quavers? How will you count them?
>
> **2** What is the key? Play the scale, thinking the note names as you play them.
>
> **3** Tap the pulse with one hand and the rhythm with the other.
>
> **4** Play a G (the first note), then hear the piece in your head. Now try singing the first two bars.
>
> **5** What does 'Andante' mean? Which words best describe the character: angry, flowing, thoughtful, ghostly?

1

> **1** Can you find two bars with the same rhythm?
>
> **2** Count two bars of $\frac{3}{4}$ aloud, then continue counting silently and clap or tap the rhythm.
>
> **3** Play the scale of the key.
>
> **4** Are any notes affected by the key signature?
>
> **5** How will you make this piece sound happy?

2

Improvise!

Improvise a 4-bar tune, then a 6-bar tune, beginning with these two bars. Keep it simple.

Compose!

Compose your own 4-bar tune beginning with these two bars. Use some patterns or ideas from the opening bars and make the final note F. Add dynamic marks and a tempo word and put in your own slurs.

Going solo!

Think about what 'playing with character' means. How can you play each
of these pieces with character? Choose two bars from each piece and use
them to begin an improvisation – play it with character.

Grade 2   Stage 1

Rhythmic exercises

6 Write your own rhythmic exercise, then clap it.

Melodic exercises

Set 1: Exploring ♩♫♩ **and C major** First play the scale and arpeggio from notation.

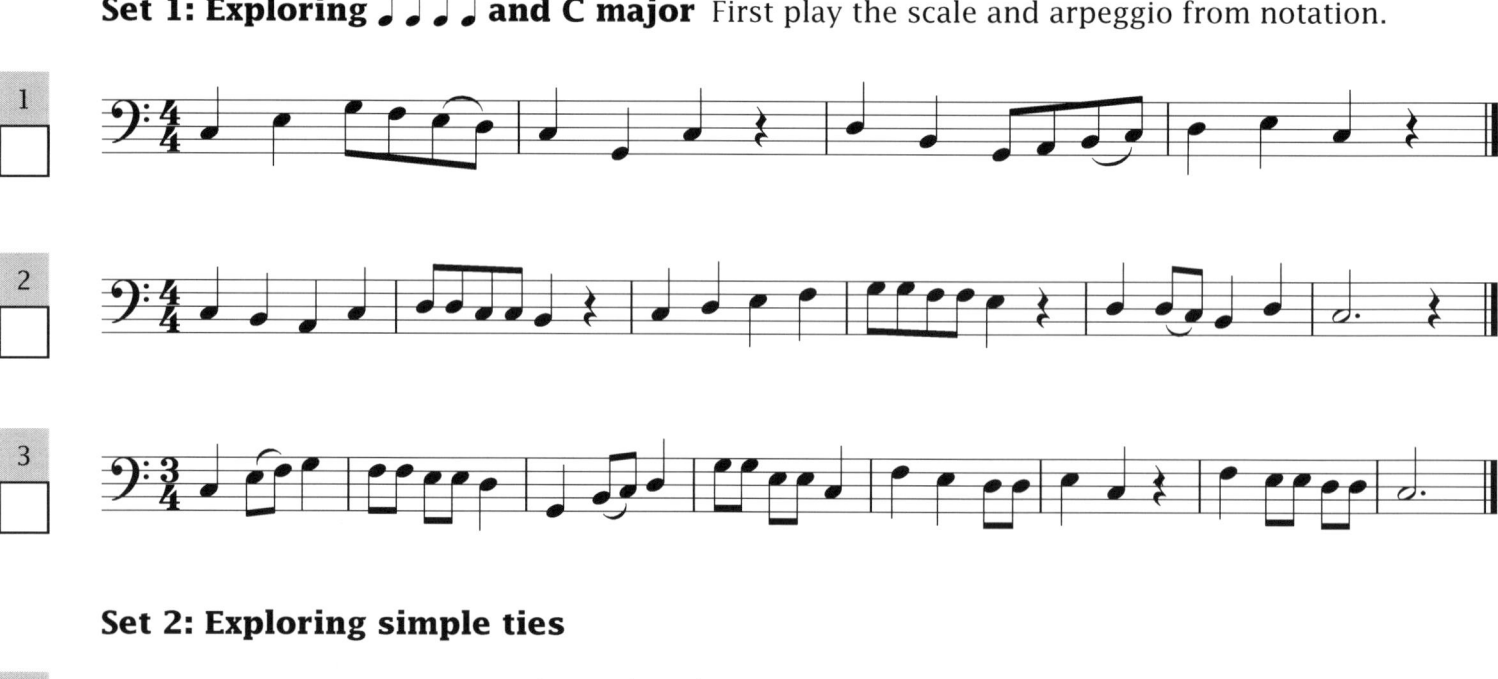

Set 2: Exploring simple ties

Prepared pieces

> **1** What is a tied note? Find the tied notes in this piece, then tap or clap bars 5–8.
>
> **2** What is the key? Play the scale, thinking of the note names as you play them.
>
> **3** Can you find any repeated rhythm patterns? Tapping the pulse with a foot, clap the rhythm of the whole piece.
>
> **4** Play a C (the first note), then hear the piece in your head as best you can.
>
> **5** What does 'Minuet' mean? How will you give the piece a 'Minuet' character?

Minuet

1

> **1** What is the character of this piece? What are the clues?
>
> **2** Find the two ties, then tap the rhythm of bars 5–8.
>
> **3** Count two bars of $\frac{4}{4}$ aloud, then continue counting silently and clap or tap the rhythm.
>
> **4** In which key is this piece? Make up a little tune in the key.
>
> **5** Play a C (the first note), then hear the piece in your head as best you can, with character.

Alla marcia

2

Improvise!

Improvise a 4-bar tune, then a 6-bar tune, beginning with these two bars.

Compose!

Compose your own 4-bar tune beginning with these two bars. Use some patterns or ideas from the opening bars and make the final note a C. Add dynamic marks, a tempo word and slurs.

Going solo!

Before playing each piece describe what you see with as much detail as possible. Mention key, melodic shapes and patterns, rhythm (particularly quaver patterns and tied notes), repeated rhythmic patterns, dynamics and character.

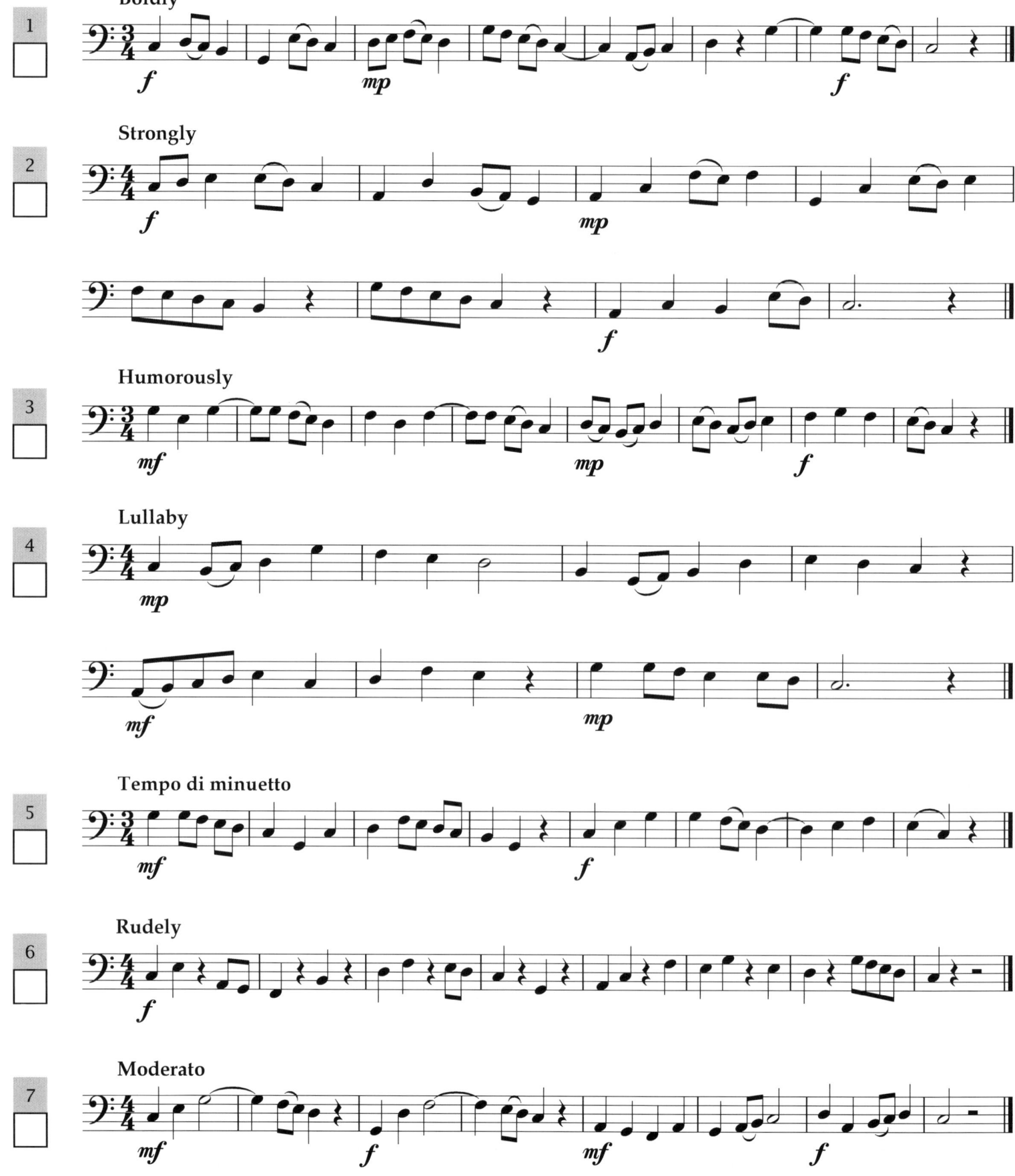

Grade 2   Stage 2

Rhythmic exercises

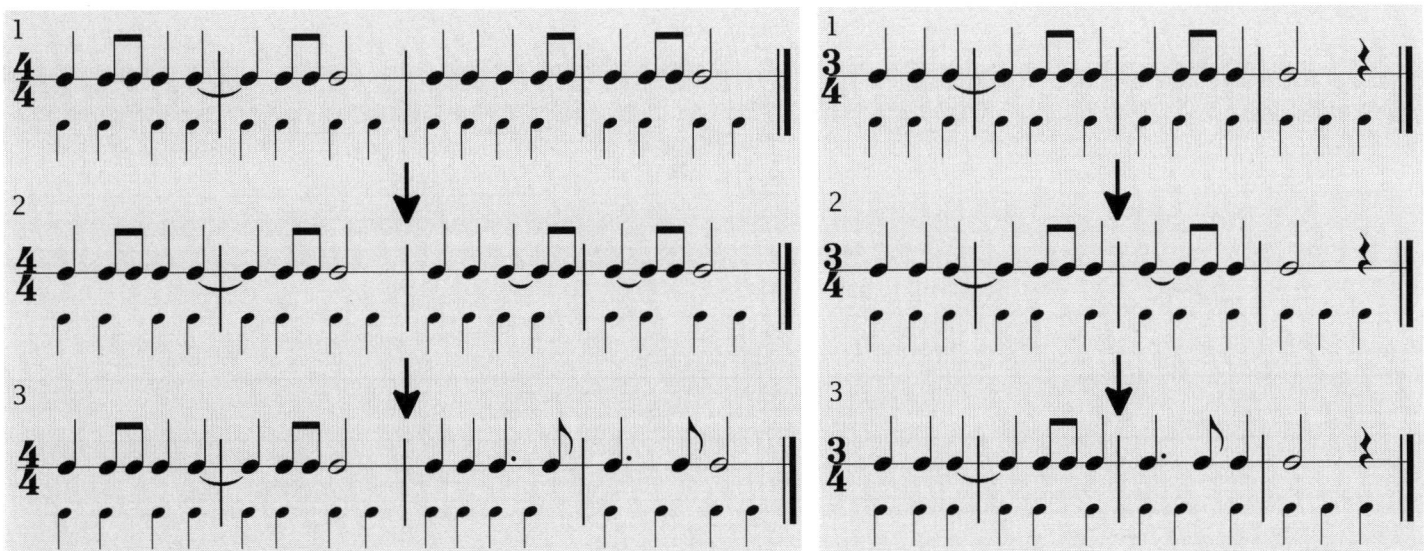

Melodic exercises

Set 1: Exploring E minor First play the scale and arpeggio from notation.
What do E minor and G major have in common?

Set 2: Exploring ♩. ♪ Feel the 4th beat strongly in this tune.

Feel the 2nd beat strongly in this one.

Prepared pieces

1 In which key is this piece? What is the relative major?

2 Describe the ♩. ♪ pattern. How will you play it accurately?

3 Can you find any repeated rhythm patterns?

4 Tapping the pulse with a foot, clap the rhythm of the whole piece. In bars that contain dotted rhythms, which beat is it important to feel strongly?

5 What does 'Cantabile' mean? How will you give the piece character?

Cantabile

1 What is the character of the piece? Why is it important to follow the dynamics?

2 How many times does the rhythm in bar 2 repeat? Tap the pulse with a foot and clap this bar.

3 Count two bars in ¾ aloud, then continue counting silently and clap or tap the rhythm of the whole piece.

4 In which key is this piece? Play the scale, then make up a little tune in the key.

5 Play the key note, then hear the piece in your head with all the dynamic markings.

Plodding

Improvise and compose!

Make up your own short piece beginning with this bar, then write it down on manuscript paper. Decide on a mood or character before you begin.

Going solo!

Study a piece for about half a minute, then, with the music out of sight,
make up a piece with broadly similar rhythmic and melodic shapes.

Grade 2 Stage 3

Staccato
Revision

Rhythmic exercises

1

2

3

Melodic exercises

1

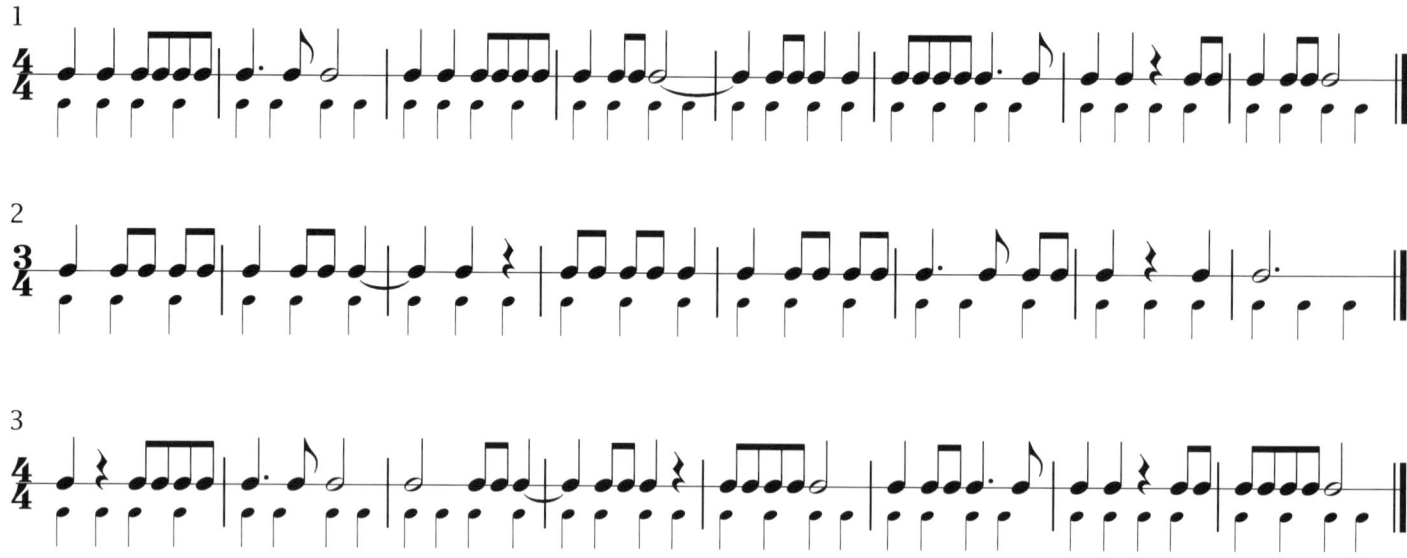

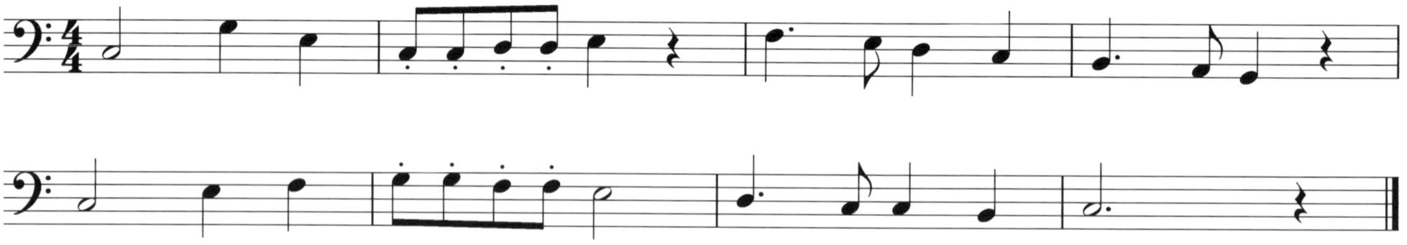

2

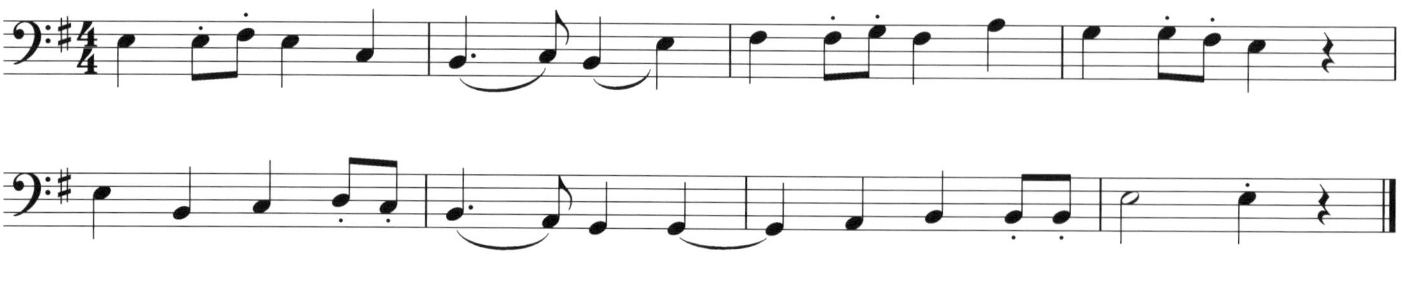

3

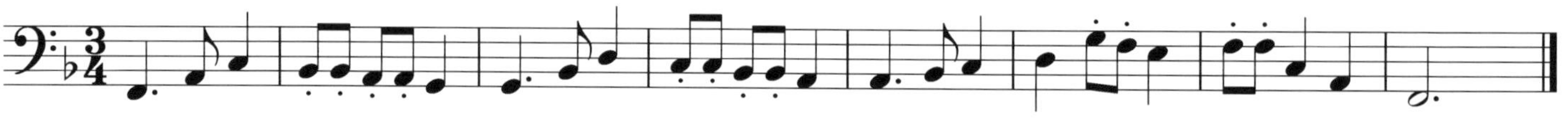

4

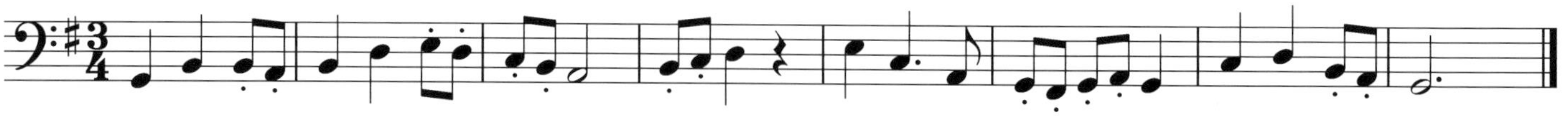

Prepared pieces

> **1** In which key is this piece? Play the scale and arpeggio, then look for any bars based on those patterns.
>
> **2** What is *staccato*? How will you play notes marked *staccato*?
>
> **3** Can you find any repeated rhythm patterns?
>
> **4** Tapping the pulse with a foot, clap the rhythm of the whole piece.
>
> **5** How will you give the piece character? Play the first note, then hear the piece in your head, with character.

> **1** What is the character of this piece? What are the clues?
>
> **2** In which key is the piece? Play a one-octave scale in this key.
>
> **3** Count two bars of 4/4 aloud, then continue counting silently and clap or tap the rhythm of the whole piece.
>
> **4** Give the piece a running commentary, mentioning rhythms, melodic patterns and markings.
>
> **5** Play an E (the key note), then hear the piece in your head as best you can, with dynamics.

Improvise and compose!

Make up your own piece beginning with this bar, then write it down on manuscript paper. Decide on a mood or character before you begin.

Going solo!

Are there any bars where you can't clap the rhythm instantly? If there are, think about them, work them out and then clap these rhythms before you play.

Grade 3 Stage 1

4-note slurs

Rhythmic exercises

1

2

3

Melodic exercises

1
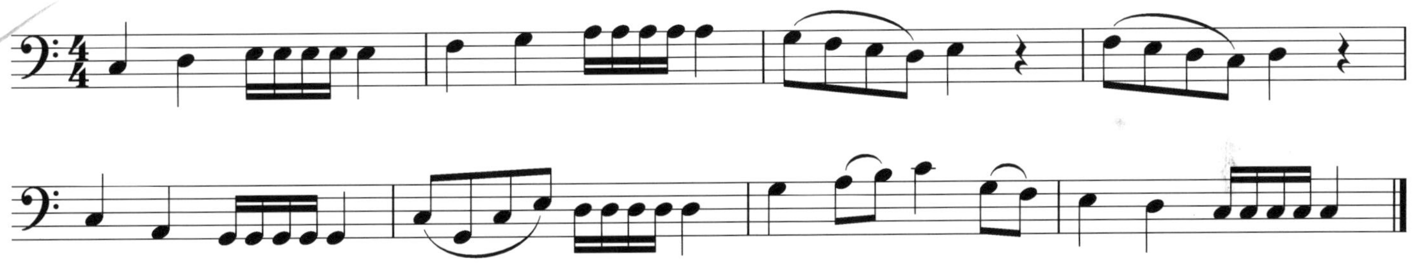

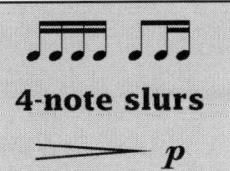

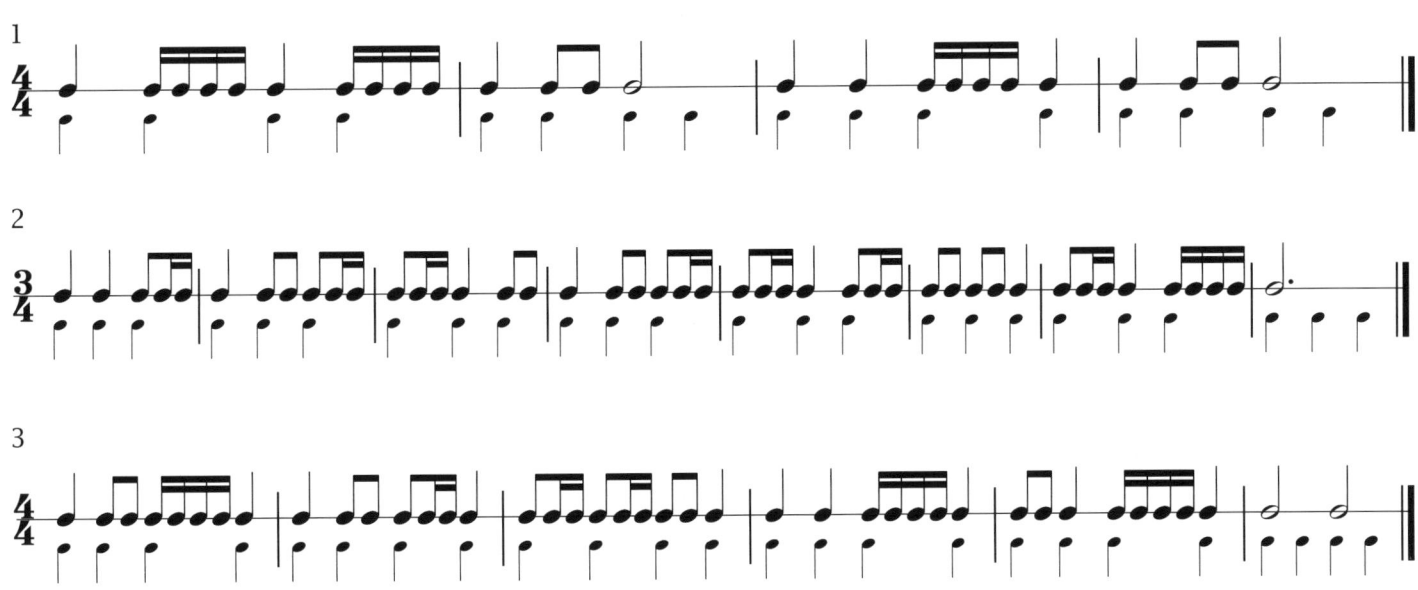

2
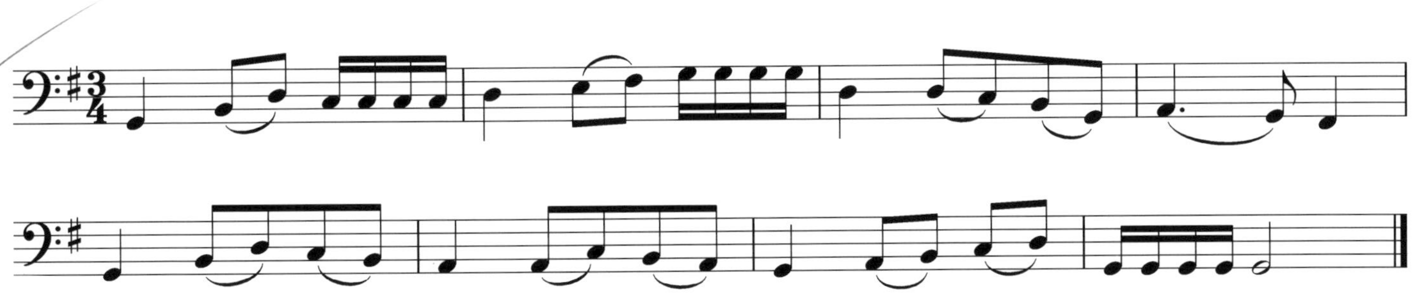

3
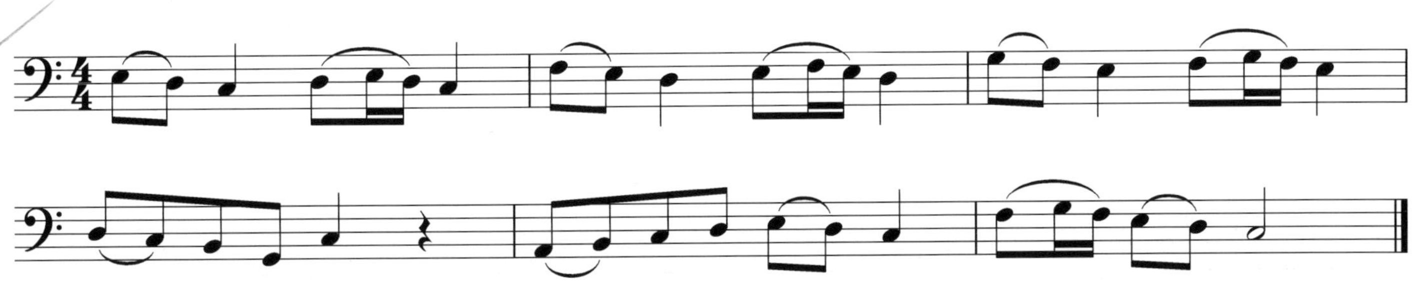

Prepared pieces

1 Look through this piece – do you feel you really understand it?

2 Are you certain of all the rhythms?

3 Play the appropriate scale first at *p*, then at *f*. Then play it with a *crescendo* on the way up and a *diminuendo* on the way down.

4 Play the first note, then hear the piece in your head as best you can, with all the markings.

5 How will you give the piece character?

1 What is the character of this piece? What are the clues?

2 Set a pulse in your mind, then sub-divide the pulse into quavers and then semiquavers. How will this help you play the first bar?

3 Count two bars of ¾ aloud, then continue counting silently and clap or tap the rhythm of the whole piece.

4 Give the piece a running commentary, mentioning rhythms, melodic patterns and markings.

5 Play a C, then study bars 5 and 6 for a few moments. Hear them in your head, then try to play them from memory.

Improvise and compose!

Make up your own piece beginning with this bar, then write it down on manuscript paper. Decide on a mood or character before you begin.

Going solo!

In each piece think about the first dynamic marking and how it relates to those
that follow. Make sure that the different markings are *really* contrasted.

Grade 3 Stage 2

A minor

Rhythmic exercises

1

2

3

Melodic exercises

Exploring A minor Play the scale and arpeggio from notation.
Which tune is in C major? How are A minor and C major related?

1

2

3

4

5

Prepared pieces

> **1** Look through this piece. Do you feel you really understand it?
>
> **2** Each phrase is two bars long, how will you make this clear in your performance?
>
> **3** Play the appropriate scale first at *mf*, then at *f*.
>
> **4** Play the first note, then hear the piece in your head, with all the musical expression.
>
> **5** How will you give the piece character?

Grazioso

> **1** How much of this piece is based on scale patterns?
>
> **2** Set a pulse in your mind, then sub-divide the pulse into quavers and then semiquavers. How will this help you play the first bar?
>
> **3** Count two bars of $\frac{3}{4}$ aloud, then continue counting silently and tap the rhythm of the whole piece.
>
> **4** Give the piece a running commentary, mentioning rhythms, melodic patterns, and markings.
>
> **5** Play an A, then study bars 1 and 2 for a few moments. Hear them in your head, then try to play them from memory.

Andantino

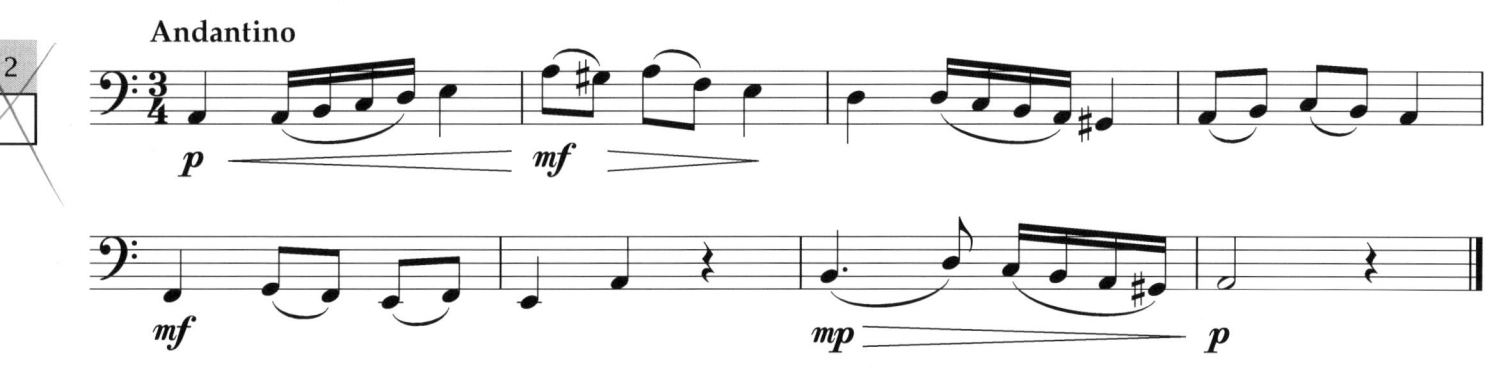

Improvise and compose!

1

Make up your own piece beginning with this phrase and write it down on manuscript paper.

2

Now compose a piece in A minor, including the ♫ rhythm. Remember to write it down.

Going solo!

Before you play each piece, choose a single bar, study it for a few seconds,
then play it from memory.

Grade 3 Stage 3

Rhythms in $\frac{3}{8}$
𝄾
Revision

Rhythmic exercises

1

2

3

Melodic exercises

1

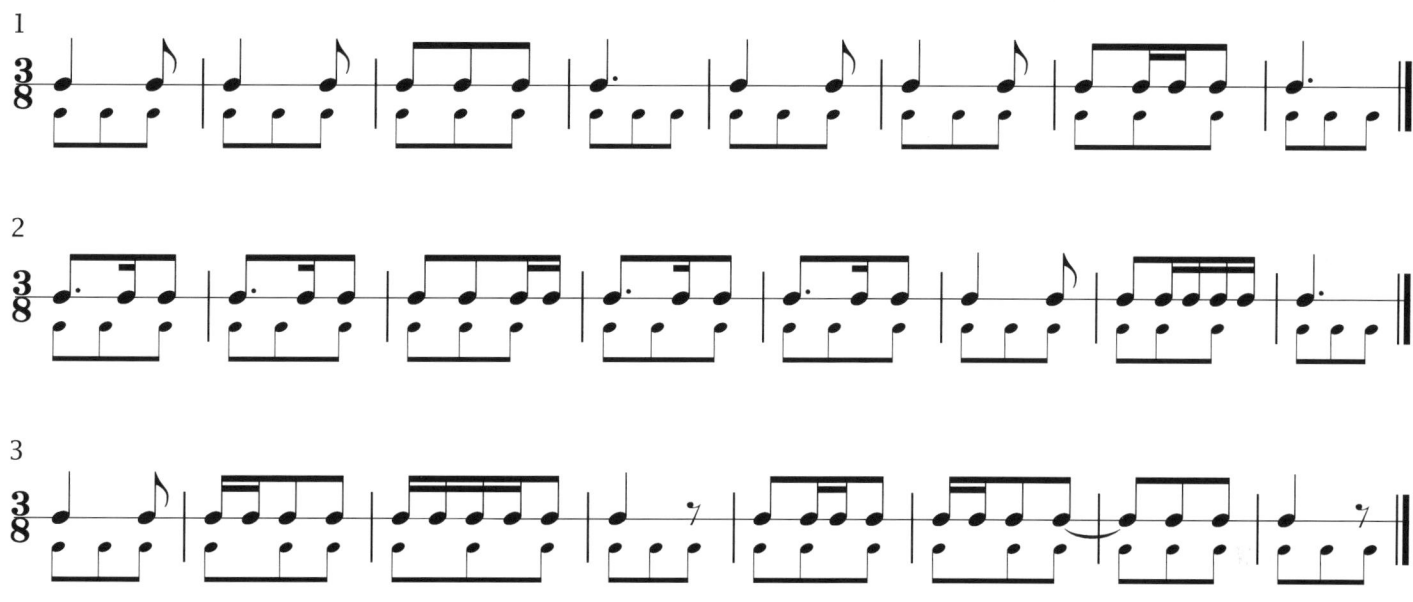

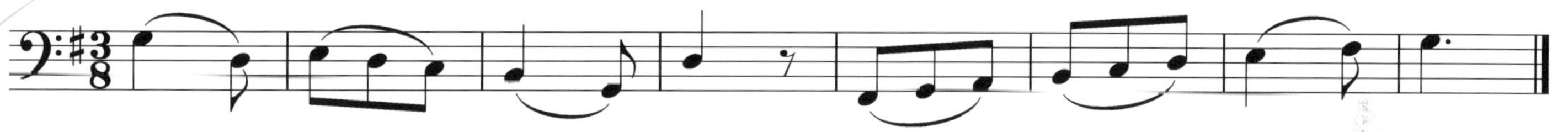

2

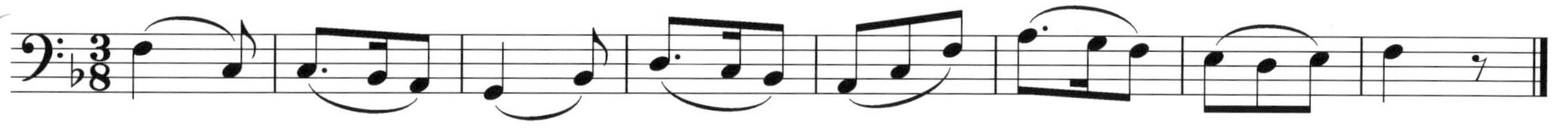

3

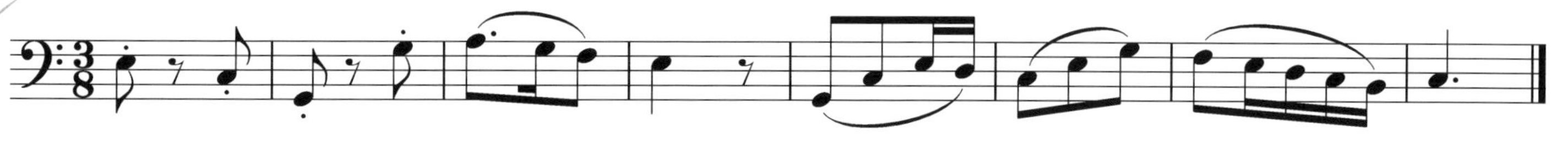

4

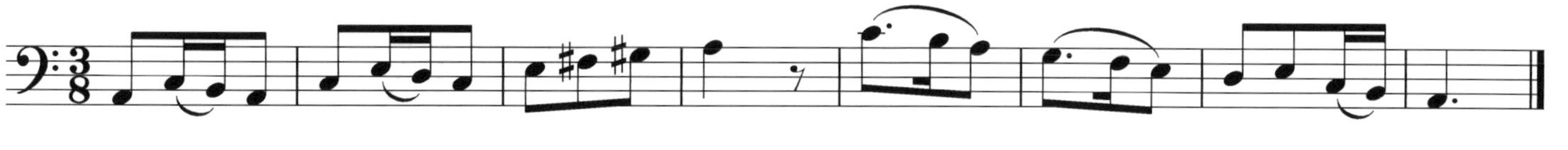

5

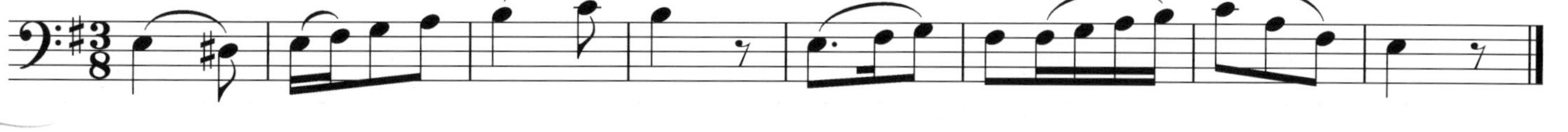

Prepared pieces

1 What does $\frac{3}{8}$ mean? How do you count in $\frac{3}{8}$?

2 In which key is this piece? Can you spot any scale and arpeggio patterns?

3 Play the scale at all three dynamic markings in the piece.

4 Play the first note, then hear the piece in your head, with all the musical expression.

5 How will you give the piece character?

1 In which key is this piece? Why is there a G♯ in bar 3?

2 How will you make sure that bar 6 is accurate?

3 Count two bars of $\frac{3}{8}$ aloud, then continue counting silently and tap the rhythm of the whole piece.

4 Do any bars share the same rhythm?

5 Play an A (the key note), then study the first two bars for a few moments. Hear them in your head, then try to play them from memory.

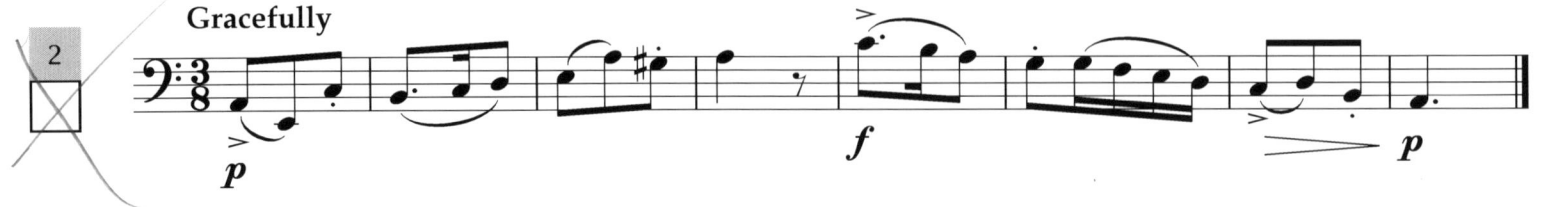

Improvise and compose!

Make up your own piece (it can be as long or short as you like) beginning with this phrase, then write it down on manuscript paper.

2 Now compose another piece, including as many $\frac{3}{8}$ patterns as you can. Remember to write it down.

Going solo!

Think about counting in a quaver pulse. Clap the rhythm of each piece before you play it.

Grade 4 Stage 1

D major
Up-beats

Rhythmic exercises

1

2

3

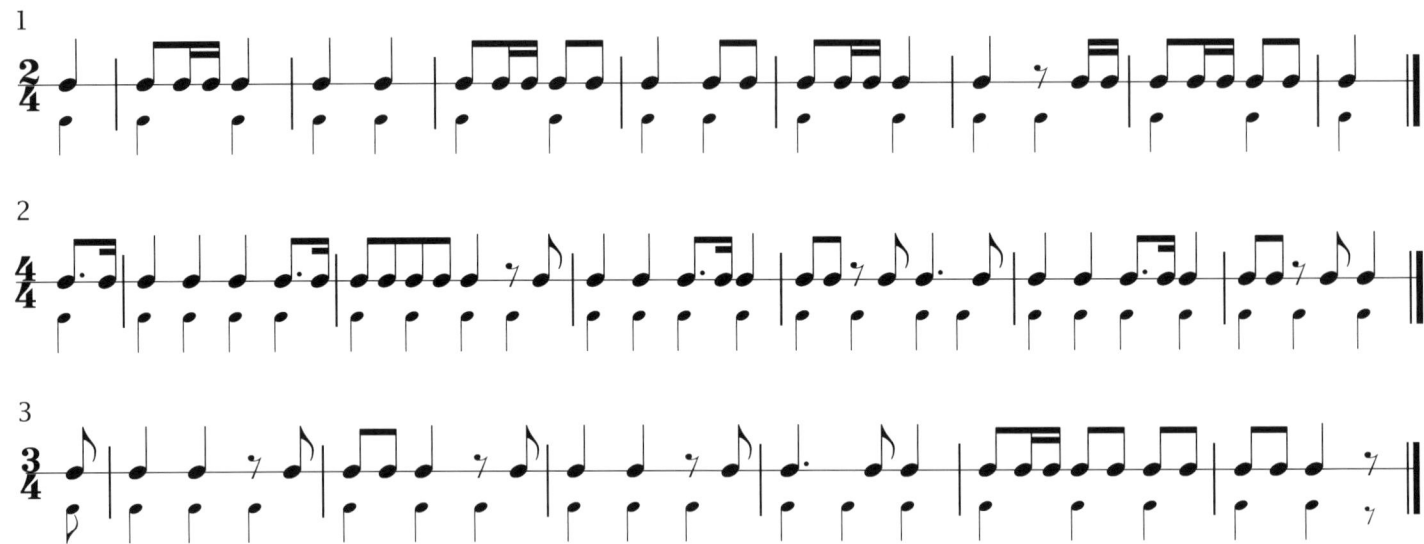

Melodic exercises

Exploring D major Play the scale and arpeggio from notation before you work through these exercises.

1
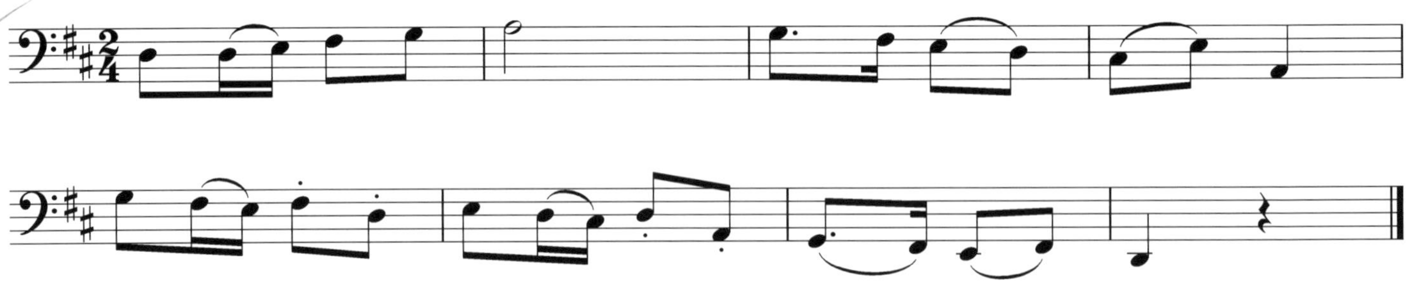

2
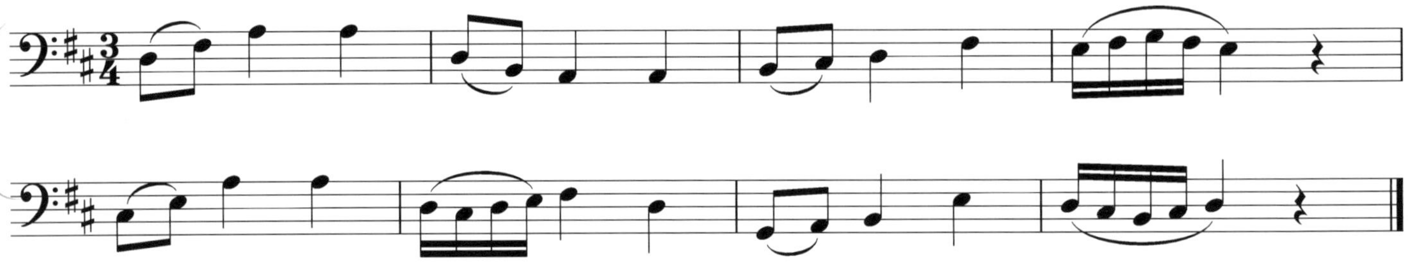

3
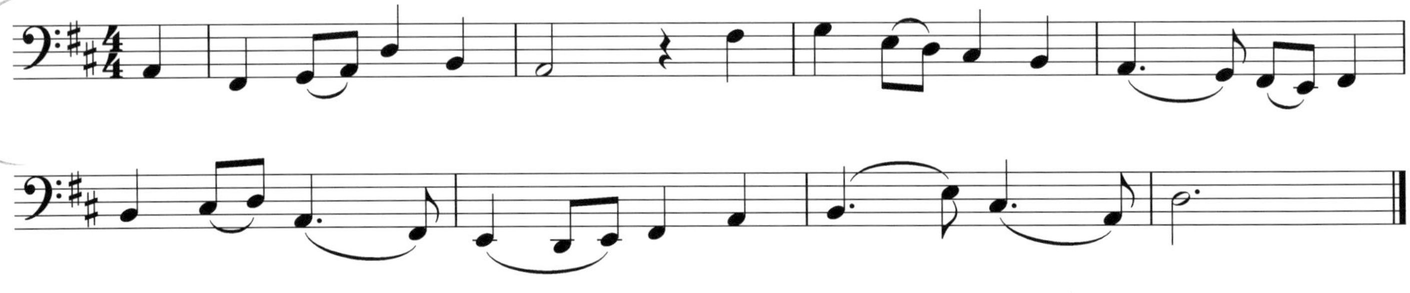

Prepared pieces

1 What is the key? Play the scale and arpeggio boldly.

2 How many bars can you find that are based on the notes of the arpeggio?

3 How many bars have similar rhythmic patterns?

4 Play a D (the first note), then hear the piece in your head.

5 How will you put some character into your performance?

1 This piece begins on an up-beat. What does this mean?

2 On your knees or a flat surface, tap the pulse with one hand and the rhythm with the other.

3 Are there any repeated rhythmic patterns?

4 Imagine all the notes affected by the key signature as being coloured red.

5 Play the first note and hear the piece in your head before you play it.

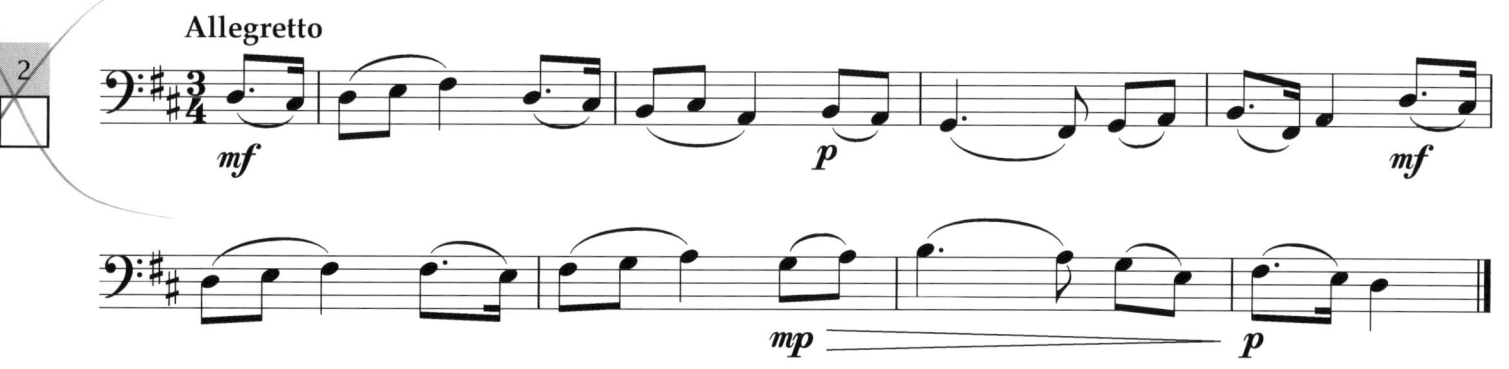

Improvise and compose!

Make up your own piece beginning with this bar,
then write it down on manuscript paper. Decide
on a mood or character before you begin.

Going solo!

Talk about each piece before you play it. Mention the key and the notes
affected by it, scales, rhythmic patterns and character.

Grade 4 Stage 2

Rhythms in $\frac{6}{8}$

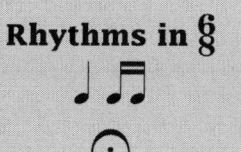

Rhythmic exercises

Always remember to count two bars in.

1

2

3

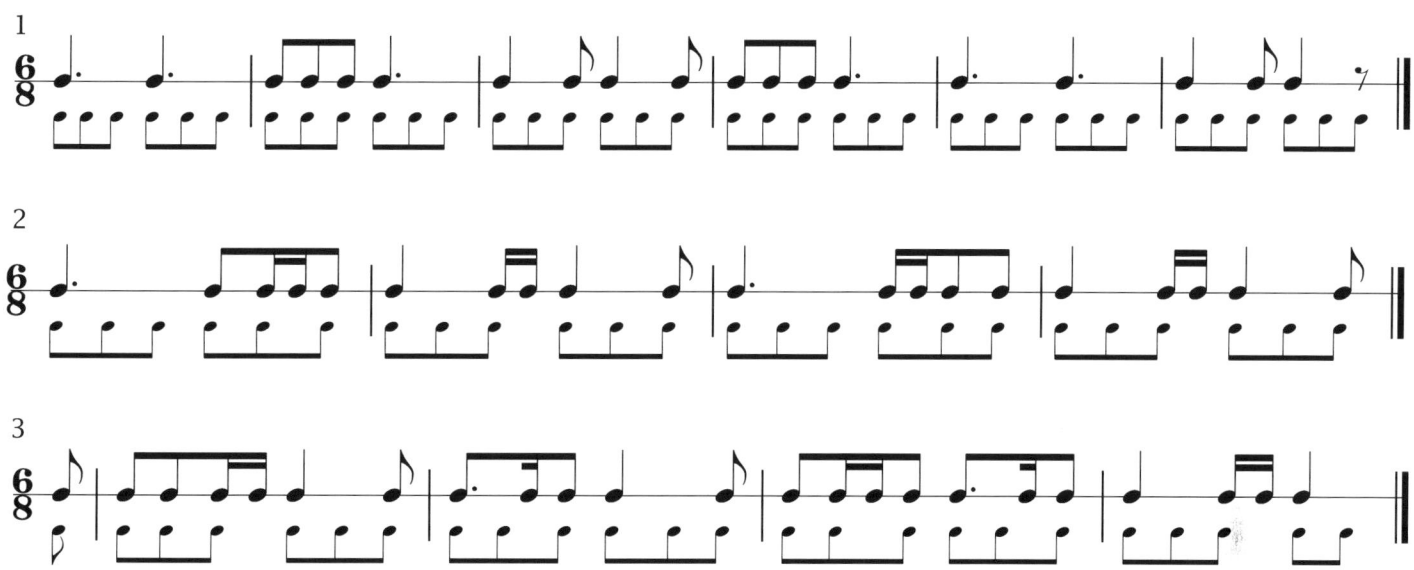

Melodic exercises

Set 1: Introducing rhythms in $\frac{6}{8}$

1

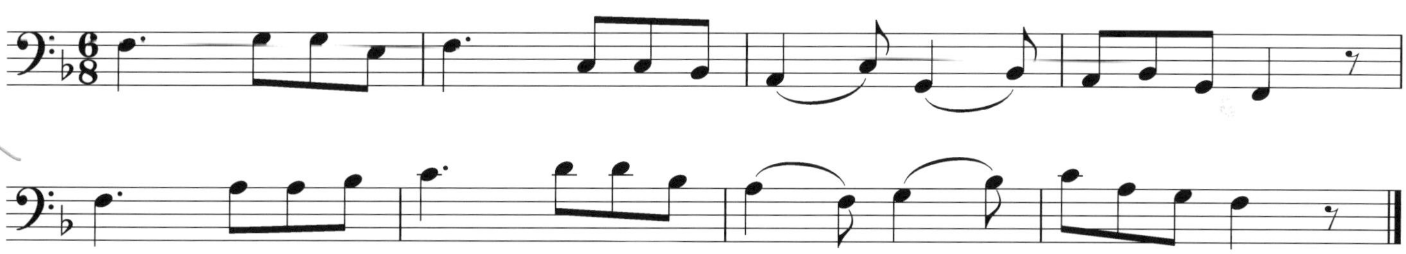

2

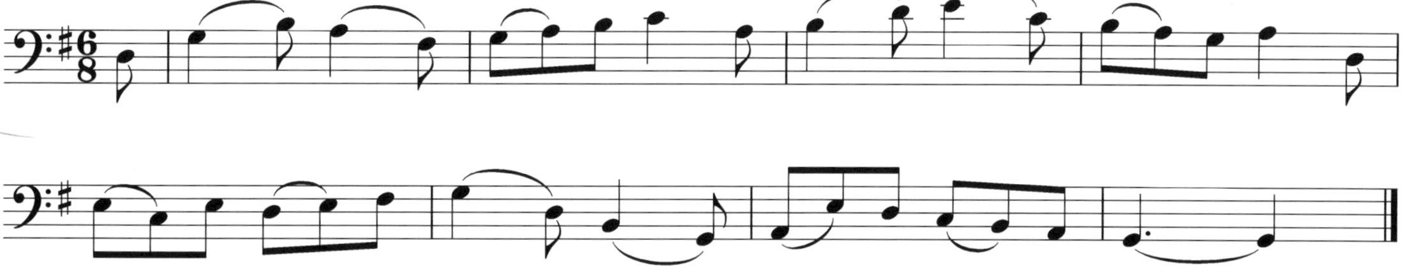

3

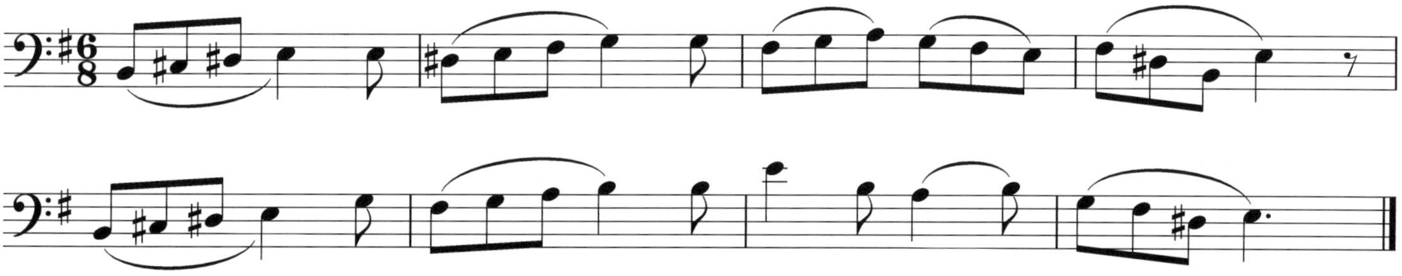

Set 2: Exploring more rhythms in $\frac{6}{8}$

Feel the pulse strongly and always give rests their full value.
Rests are often good moments to look ahead.

Improvise!

Improvise a tune beginning with these notes. It can be as short or as long
as you like. Give it character. Think about what's coming next as you play.

Compose!

Compose your own 4-bar tune beginning with this bar. Use the idea of the
first bar in your melody. Make the final note a D, then play your tune.

Prepared pieces

1 How will you count this piece? What does the time signature tell you?

2 What is the key? Can you find any scale patterns?

3 Play the highest and lowest notes. What are their names?

4 Play a D (the first note), then hear the piece in your head.

5 How will you give this piece character?

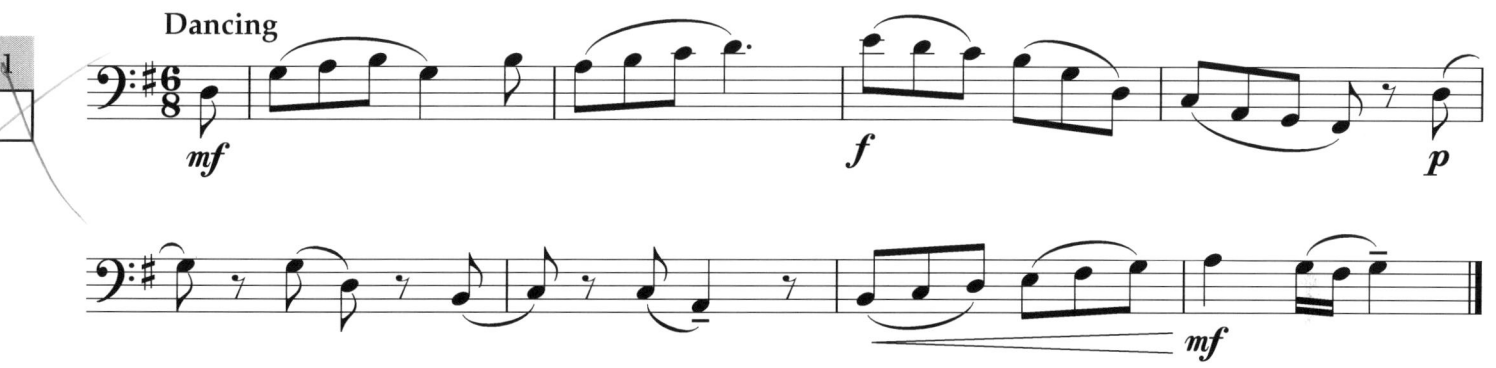

1 What pulse will you feel? How will you play the first bar with the correct
   note lengths?

2 Tapping the pulse, hear the rhythm in your head. Then, clap the rhythm and
   tap the pulse with a foot at the same time.

3 Are there any repeated rhythmic patterns?

4 Play a C (the first note), then hear the piece in your head.

5 How will you give energy to your performance?

Going solo!

Before playing each piece, choose two bars and study them silently for half a minute,
then play them from memory.

Grade 4 Stage 3

D minor

Revision

Rhythmic exercises

Always remember to count two bars in.

Melodic exercises

Exploring D minor Which major key is related to D minor and why? Play a D minor scale and arpeggio and its related major patterns from notation and memory.

1

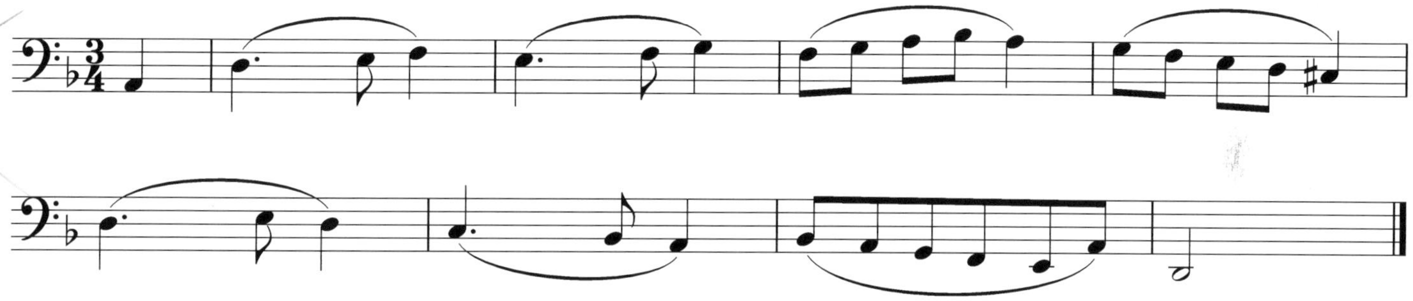

2

3

Prepared pieces

1 Think through the rhythm of the whole piece sensing a semiquaver subdivision.
   Then think it through again sensing a crotchet pulse.

2 What is the key? Play the scale, thinking the note names as you play them.

3 Look for repeated rhythm patterns.

4 Play an A (the first note), then hear the piece in your head as best you can.

5 How will you give your performance character?

1 How will you place the two semiquavers in bars 1, 2, 5 and 6 accurately?

2 Tapping the pulse, hear the rhythm in your head. Then clap the rhythm and tap
   the pulse with your foot at the same time.

3 Compare bars 1 and 2 in detail.

4 Give the piece a running commentary, mentioning rhythm patterns, the melodic
   shape and any markings.

5 How will you make the piece flow? Why are the dynamic markings so important?

Improvise and compose!

Make up your own piece beginning with this
phrase, then write it down on manuscript paper.
Decide on a mood or character before you begin.

Going solo!

Look at each piece carefully before you play it. If there are any passages you don't understand, discuss these with your teacher. Don't play until you feel confident.

Grade 5 Stage 1

B♭ major
G minor
Syncopation

Rhythmic exercises

1

2

3

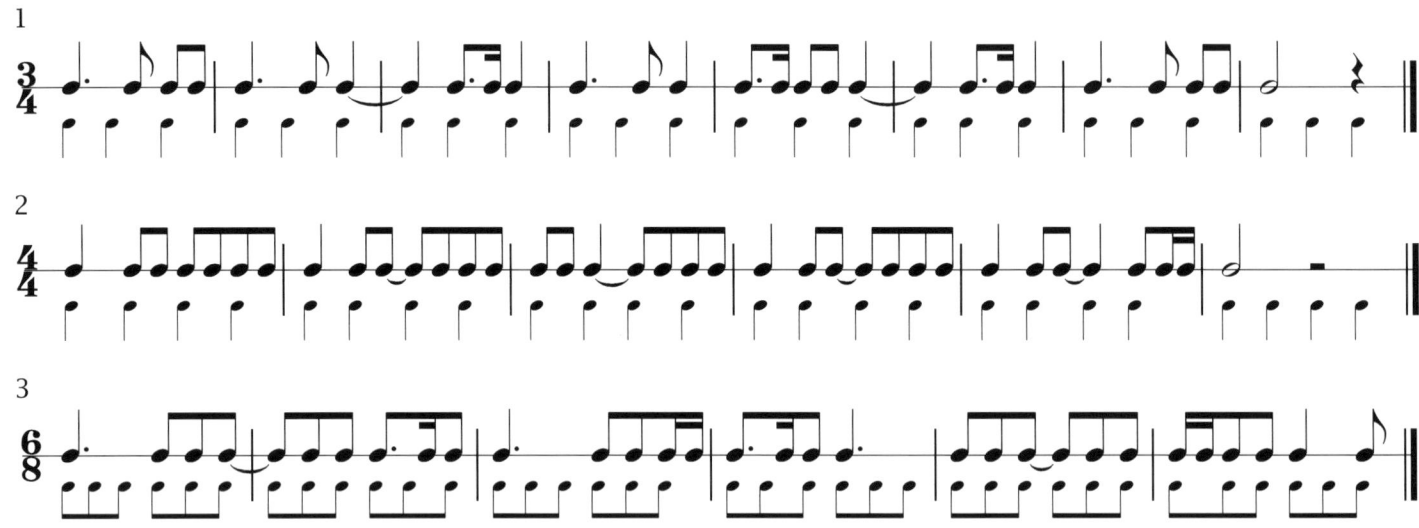

Melodic exercises

Exploring B♭ major and G minor How are these two keys related? Play the scales and arpeggios from notation.

1

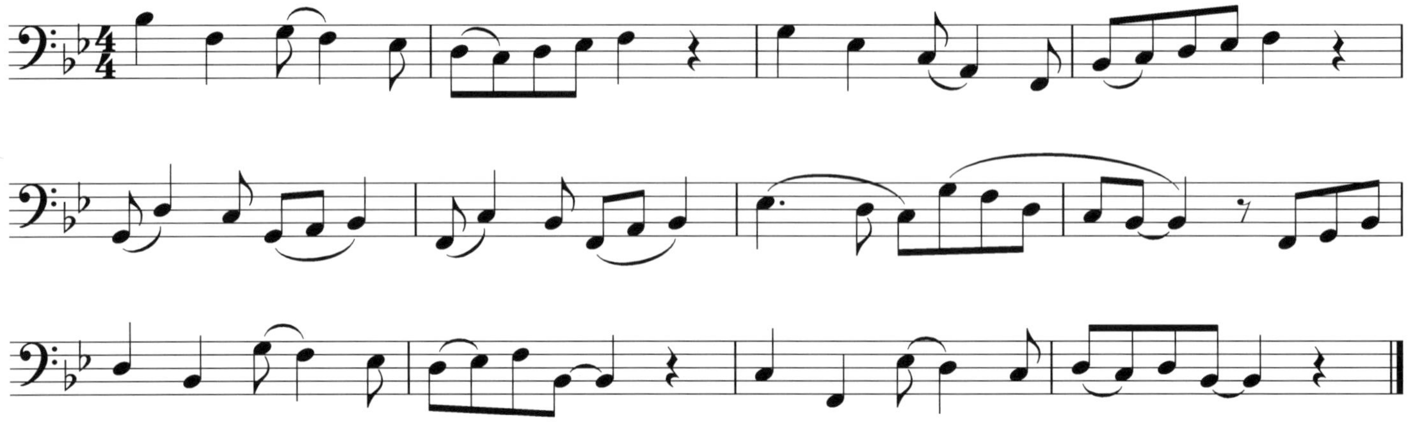

2

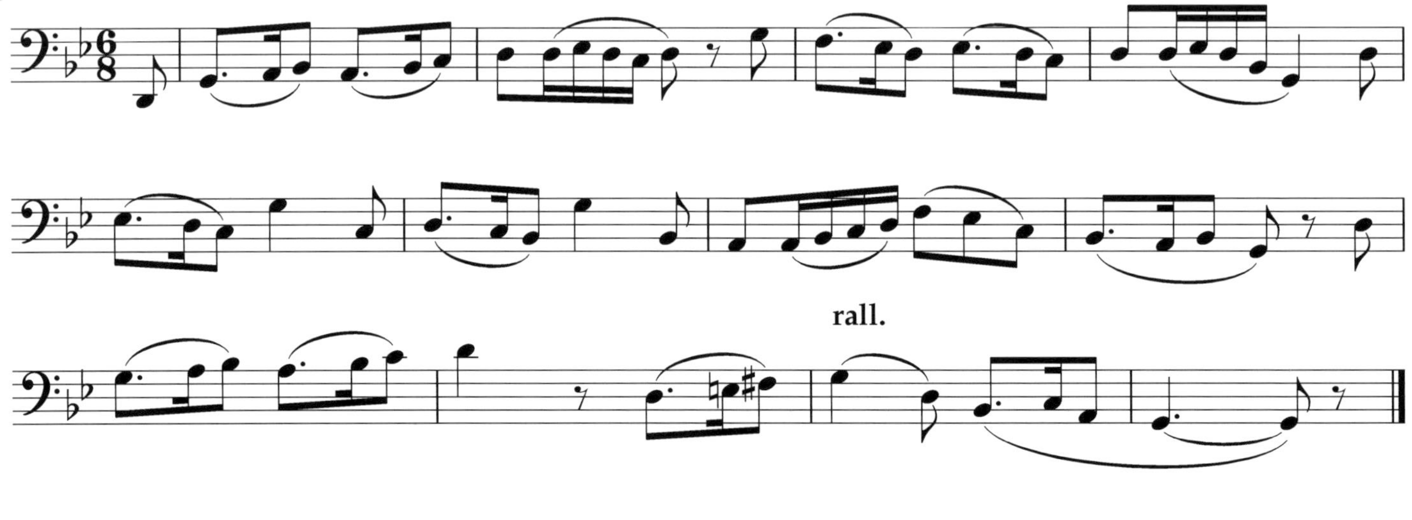

Prepared pieces

1 What does syncopation mean? Find an example in this piece and explain it carefully.

2 What is the key? Play the scale and arpeggio from notation.

3 Give the piece a running commentary, mentioning melodic and rhythmic patterns.

4 Play a B♭ (the first note), then hear the piece in your head as best you can.

5 How will you give the piece character?

Cool blues style

1 What is the character of this piece? What are the clues?

2 Find all the ties, then tap bars 1–4.

3 Count two bars of ⁶⁄₈ aloud, then continue counting silently and clap or tap the rhythm.

4 In which key is this piece? Make up a little tune in the key.

5 Play a D (the first note), then hear the piece in your head as best you can, with character.

Flowing

Going solo!

Exaggerate all the dynamics and other markings in these pieces. Think about shaping the phrases too. Play with confidence and a sense that each performance is a special event.

Grade 5 Stage 2

A major
E♭ major
pp* and *ff

Rhythmic exercises

1

2

3

Melodic exercises

Exploring A major and E♭ major Play the appropriate scale and arpeggio many times from notation and memory until you are really thinking *in the key*.

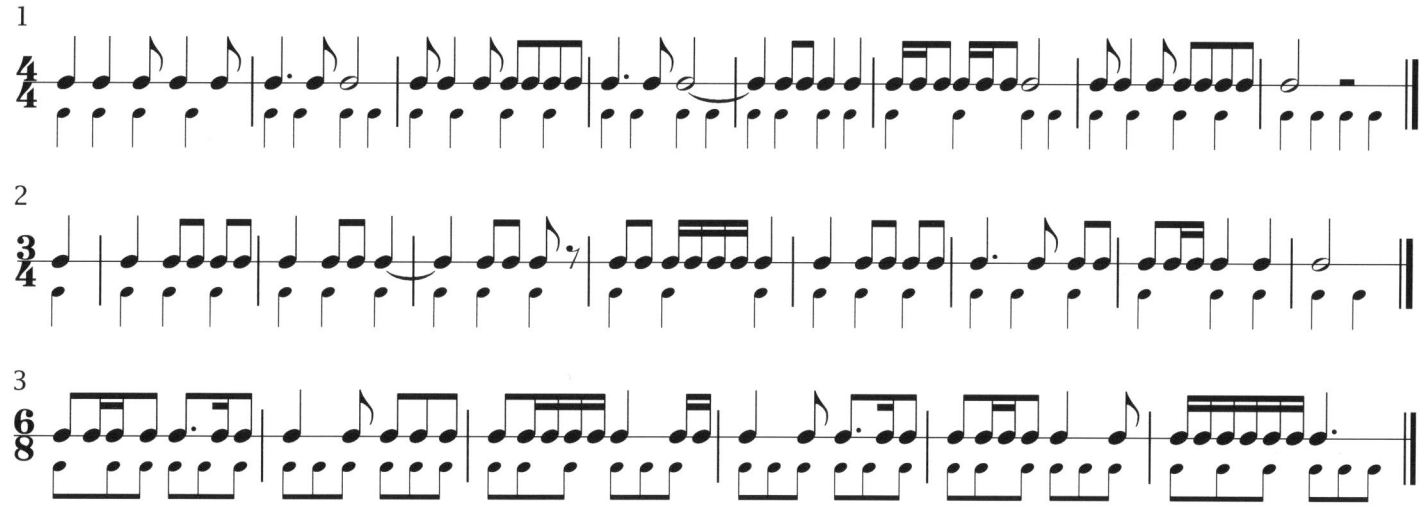

1

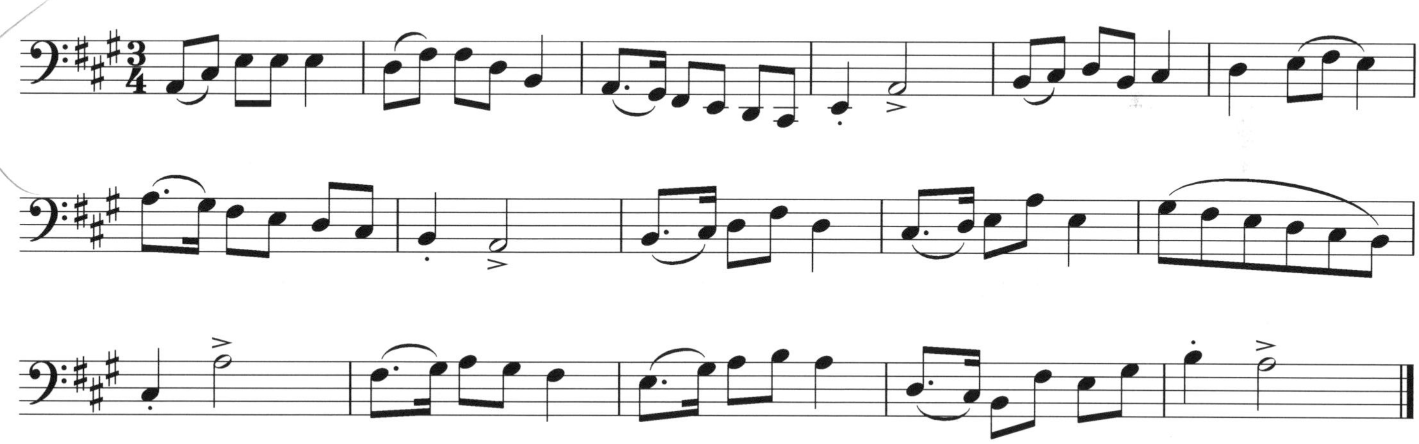

2

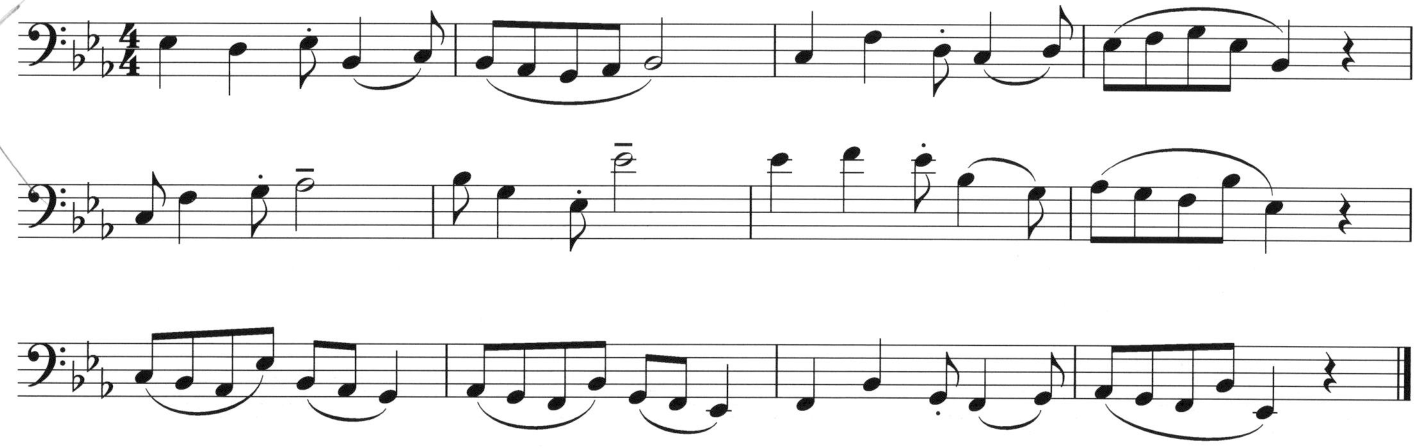

Prepared pieces

1 In which key is this piece? Why does it have three sharps?

2 How does the rhythm of each bar relate to a quaver pulse?

3 Can you find any repeated rhythm patterns?

4 Tapping the pulse with a foot, clap the rhythm of the whole piece.

5 How will you give the piece character?

1 What is the character of this piece? Why is it important to follow the dynamic markings?

2 Can you describe the shape of this piece?

3 Counting silently, clap or tap the rhythm of the whole piece.

4 In which key is this piece? Play a two-octave scale then make up a little tune in the key.

5 Play an E♭ (the first note), then hear the piece in your head as best you can, with all the dynamic markings.

Going solo!

Study each piece for about half a minute, then with the music out of sight,
make up a piece with broadly similar rhythmic and melodic shapes.

Grade 5 Stage 3

**B minor
Revision**

Rhythmic exercises

Choose a pattern, look at it for a few seconds and then cover it up.
Clap it from memory and then look to see if you were correct.

Melodic exercises

Exploring B minor Play the scale and arpeggio from notation before you begin these exercises.

Prepared pieces

1 In which key is this piece? Explain the accidentals in bars 3 and 4.

2 How will you be sure that the semiquavers in bar 1 will be accurate?

3 Can you find any repeated rhythm or scale patterns?

4 Tapping the pulse with a foot, clap the rhythm of the whole piece.

5 How will you give the piece character? How will you bring it to life?

1 What is the character of this piece? Why is it important to follow the dynamic markings?

2 How will you play the staccato and accented notes?

3 Count two bars of $\frac{3}{4}$ aloud, then continue counting silently and clap or tap the rhythm of the whole piece.

4 In which key is this piece? Play a two-octave scale and arpeggio.

5 Play an A (the first note), then hear the piece in your head as best you can, with all the dynamic markings.

Going solo!

Bloomsbury House, 74–77 Great Russell Street, London WC1B 3DA
Cover and page design by Susan Clarke
Printed in England by Caligraving Ltd

ISBN10: 0-571-54026-0
EAN13: 978-0-571-54026-6

With thanks to Emily Newman and Tom Dent.